The Sun Book of Short Stories

Foreword by Jane Moore

BANTAM BOOKS

LONDON • TORONTO • SYDNEY • AUCKLAND • JOHANNESBURG

TRANSWORLD PUBLISHERS
61–63 Uxbridge Road, London W5 5SA,
a division of The Random House Group Ltd
www.booksattransworld.co.uk

THE SUN
BOOK OF SHORT STORIES
A BANTAM BOOK: 9780553818826

First publication in Great Britain, published by
arrangement with The Sun newspaper
Bantam edition published 2007

Compilation copyright © Transworld Publishers 2007
For copyright details of individual stories, see page opposite

Quick ReadsTM used under licence

Addresses for Random House Group Ltd companies outside the UK
can be found at: www.randomhouse.co.uk
The Random House Group Ltd Reg. No. 954009

The Random House Group Limited makes every effort to ensure that the
papers used in its books are made from trees that have been legally
sourced from well-managed and credibly certified forests. Our paper
procurement policy can be found at:
www.randomhouse.co.uk/paper.htm

Set in Stone Serif by SX Composing DTP, Rayleigh, Essex.
Printed and bound in Great Britain by
Cox & Wyman Ltd, Reading, Berkshire.

2 4 6 8 10 9 7 5 3

CONTENTS

FOREWORD

Everyone *thinks* they can write a short story or even a novel.

After all, they think, I'm really good at *telling* a funny or interesting tale. How hard can it be to put it down on paper and get the same result?

But when they actually try, they soon realize that it's very difficult indeed. You don't have gestures or facial expressions to help you out. You don't have the benefit of eye contact with the person you're speaking to. You have to pull them in to your story purely by what you write on the page, the way you create your characters and give them a realistic plot or twist. When you're writing a short story, this is doubly hard because you have so little time to capture the reader's imagination. As a result, your writing has to be sharp and to the point, well paced in a very small space. Believe me, it's tough to do.

I really admire anyone who can write a compelling short story, so I was thrilled to be one of the judges for *The Sun*'s short story competition 'Get Britain Reading'. It's designed to tie in with World Book Day and to champion the cause of promoting literacy. The idea was to find brilliant, unpublished writers. We were overwhelmed by the tens of thousands who entered short stories of a very high standard. Some were skilled at writing punchy prose with twists and turns, others preferred a slower style, drawing the reader in to a detailed moment in time. It was an extremely tricky job to come up with a shortlist! But after much deliberation, our panel of judges picked the best from the Under 16 and Over 16 categories, many of which are printed in this book.

I have little doubt that some of the short story writers you see here today will become the bestselling novelists of tomorrow. Enjoy!

Jane Moore

The Sun Book of Short Stories

BALL GAMES

Francesca Bardsley

AMIRA WASN'T ALLOWED TO talk to strangers. In those dark days the city was dangerous, especially for a nine-year-old girl. Even one who knew where it was safe to go and when to run and hide.

But Khaled was no stranger. Everyone knew him. His smile, his swagger, his roll-up cigarette in the corner of his mouth. He would crack a joke with her father. Offer a respectful comment on her mother's cooking. Amira knew she was safe when she was with Khaled.

She was playing with a group of children one day. They were in what had once been the schoolyard, before it had been destroyed. Khaled joined them. There was a hoop attached to what remained of the school wall. He challenged the girls and boys to throw a rock through the hoop.

Amira's eyes lit up and she clapped her hands

1

together, laughing, as her rock went straight through. It just clipped the rusty metal ring as it fell back to earth. No one else even came close.

'Well done, little one!' said Khaled. 'You are better than all these big boys.'

He searched through his pocket and produced a brown paper bag full of sticky pastries.

'Take this,' he said. 'You deserve it.'

Amira often saw Khaled at the schoolyard after that and showed him how well she could throw. He told her she was getting better. Every time she cleared the hoop, he gave her something. They were small things. Sometimes extra rice to take home to her mother. Sometimes flour or spices. Sometimes little sweet things Amira could keep for herself.

He started giving her tips. Telling her to pull her arm back and focus her eyes before letting go. Soon she could make the hoop every time. It seemed natural when Khaled suggested they go in search of new targets.

They practised together often, always in the safe neighbourhoods. But Amira felt no fear when she was with Khaled. He had told her she was better than the boys. She trusted him. Besides, no one messed with Khaled.

Sometimes he would make marks on walls or on the ground. Amira would land the rocks, or whatever they had found to throw that day, on his mark.

Once they found a burnt-out truck. Amira would have been afraid to go near it but Khaled told her it was safe. They used that for her to aim at. At first Amira couldn't throw her rock through the empty windows where the glass had been. But soon she had mastered that too.

Khaled strolled up to Amira one day when she was at home. She was surprised. Usually they would meet at the schoolyard, and she had seen him there only yesterday. 'Come with me,' he said. 'I have a new thing for you to try. It will be a little harder, but I'm sure you can do it. You are such a clever girl.'

She followed Khaled, but became uneasy when they started leaving her familiar neighbourhood. He could see her mood and laughed at her. 'Don't be such a frightened little mouse, you're with Khaled.'

She continued walking but held her hands tightly together behind her back, wishing away the bad people her mother and father had warned her about.

They approached a courtyard. There was nobody to be seen but the atmosphere felt different – tense and dangerous. Amira shook it from her mind. Khaled would never take her to a place that wasn't safe.

He showed her the day's challenge, pressing a small, hard round thing into her hand. It felt different from the usual rocks but Amira did not really notice. She fixed her mind on the throw, wondering what he would give her afterwards.

Amira narrowed her eyes, squinting at the small window on the other side of the courtyard. Khaled waited a few yards away, behind a pillar. He smiled as she pulled her arm back and threw the dark, metallic object at her target. It was heavier than the rocks and balls of string she had practised with. But her aim was perfect. It sailed through the window.

A few seconds later, heat and fire surged past Amira's frail body. She was thrown on to her back. The air was thick with acrid black smoke.

4

She was on the ground, unable to breathe, her eyes were stinging and watering. Blood trickled down the side of her face. Her arms and legs were numb and did not move. Amira could not hear the sound of the debris falling down around her. Just a strange, far-off ringing in her ears. Soon even that faded as she drifted away, not feeling the pain any more, not feeling anything. Bleeding. Dying.

Khaled slipped away, unseen, unheard. A crumpled brown cigarette drooped out of one corner of his mouth. As he walked away from the scene of bloody carnage, he smiled a half-smile. Rifle slung casually over one shoulder, he lit his cigarette.

A LIVING

Gavin Bell

I SIT ON THE edge of the bath. I'm smoking and gazing at the straight razor resting on the sink. I wonder what an old thing like that is doing in an early-twenty-first-century hotel room.

My dad used a straight razor. Every day of his life, no matter what, he always shaved himself carefully. I remember the only time I saw him not looking his best. He had lost his job and had been out of the house for three days, drinking whisky and wearing the same clothes. But still, from the neck up he could have been on a poster for Gillette. Right after that he got a better job and everything was fine again. My dad was a good guy. I prefer the stubbly look personally.

I take a last drag on the cigarette and toss the butt into the toilet, hearing a satisfying fizzle as it hits the water.

I was fourteen when I had my first cigarette.

A Marlboro Light, which was given to me by a girl I was trying to impress at a party. I was expecting to cough like everyone says you will when you first try smoking. But it didn't happen. I just got a weird feeling in my chest. I thought that the taste was somehow like bad coffee. A few more tries and I got to like the bad-coffee taste.

Things didn't work out with the girl, but I did find a partner for life that night.

It's funny how every little thing makes you look back at your life at a time like this.

I remember the first time I got laid . . .

Just like smoking, it wasn't how I thought it would be. I mean, it's meant to be terrible, isn't it, your first time? Something you put behind you quickly and try to build on. But it wasn't. I was sixteen, her name was Abigail. We had a date at a fairground. Everything that could go wrong did go wrong. First I lost my wallet, then she accidentally spilled her Coke all over me. I walked her to the bus stop. But we both realized that neither of us wanted the night to end.

She led me by the hand up the grassy slope behind the fair. We kissed for a while. I still remember how intense everything felt. Even the scent of burning hamburgers and the distant, steady beat of bad dance music. We made love on grass that was still slightly warm from the daytime.

I never saw her again. Your first time's meant to be the worst, but not for me. I've been chasing that feeling all my life.

I check my watch. 11.47. Not long now.

I glance around the bathroom. Aside from the straight razor, it's exactly the same bathroom you find in four-star hotel rooms across the world. White-tiled floor. White ceramic bath, sink and toilet. Chrome towel rack with towels which are nice but not *too* nice. Some dull art on the wall. In this case it's a watercolour painting of a naked woman. She's sitting with her back to us at the edge of a pier, looking out at a deep blue lake under a light blue sky. I've seen worse, actually.

I used to be pretty good at painting. Painted pretty much every day, back when I was a teenager. I was into expressionism, though. Stuff that showed what mood I was in and what I was thinking about. Not naked women and lakes. My high school art teacher wanted me to keep studying it. I wasn't interested. I preferred girls and cars and work. I was growing up. I guess it happens to everyone.

There I go again, even bad art makes me think about my life.

I realize it's almost time now and stand up, smoothing out the creases in my suit as I rise. I walk over to the mirror and run a finger through my hair. Then I stroke the stubble I've grown. I could do with a shave, but I don't want to use the straight razor. Besides, I don't have the time.

I hear the sound of a key-card slotting into the hotel room door. Quickly I turn the bathroom light out, pushing the bathroom door slightly so I can see out. The room door opens, light spilling across the typical four-star hotel room. A man in a suit walks in. He's looking tired. His suit is nice. Not as nice as mine, but pretty good.

I take the gun out of my shoulder holster and quietly screw on the silencer. I open the bathroom door. The guy looks startled. I shoot him three times in the chest and put another bullet in his head. As he's falling to the floor he still has the surprised look on his face.

I unscrew the silencer and stare blankly at his

body. Dark arterial blood is already seeping into the carpet. This seems to be the only thing tonight that doesn't make me think about my life.

I don't know why he had to die. I don't even know who he is. I don't know if he has a wife, or kids. I don't know what his dad did.

I don't know whether he ever thought about the first girl he made love to and never saw again.

I just know that a brown envelope full of money will be pushed under my door tomorrow morning.

I hate this.

But it's a living.

HENRY

Elizabeth Brassington

'HERE, LET ME DO it. You're useless!'

My wife snatched the knife from my hand and briskly cut the tough tape. It bound a strangely shaped parcel. A satisfied smile curved her lips as she peeled back the paper. She lifted out what seemed to be a folded air bed. 'Don't just stare,' she snapped. 'Fetch me your bicycle pump.'

As she pumped air into the strange object, I saw with surprise that it was taking on a human form.

She paused to rest her aching arms.

'Let me,' I offered.

'I can manage quite well without you,' she rasped, slapping my hand off the pump handle.

She gazed with admiration as the figure slowly grew to full size. In our tiny kitchen he towered over my puny height of five foot nothing. He looked handsome and smart with his green vinyl suit and firm jaw.

'For the car,' she snapped at me again. 'I saw him advertised in the paper. He's going to sit next to me and frighten off muggers.'

I smiled. My wife would frighten off muggers without the help of a dummy.

'Isn't he a pet?' she said, beaming at him. 'I shall call him Henry.'

My wife was very pleased with Henry. I stayed at home and did the housework, while Henry went out in the car with her. In the evenings, he sat in my armchair, safely away from the fire. I shifted about on the hard kitchen chair, glaring at his snooty profile and smug smile.

'Don't you dare complain,' said my wife. 'He's more use than you are. Anyway, he falls off if I put him on that wooden chair.'

At Christmas, my wife bought me a set of kitchen skewers and a potato-peeler. Henry got a checked cap, a long tartan scarf and a smart pair of driving gloves.

'He deserves them,' she said, 'you're just useless!'

A great surge of anger rose up in me. How I hated them both, especially Henry with his vain, well-bred smile! I grabbed a skewer from the kitchen and plunged it into the tough vinyl of his back. There was a pop, and then a hissing sound, as Henry began to deflate. I squeezed his neck and beat on his chest to hurry things up.

My wife screamed with hatred. 'How dare you?' she yelled. 'He's twice the man you are!' But clearly, by this time, he was not. He had rapidly shrunk down to my own puny size. 'Save him, save him!' she groaned. She wrenched out the skewer and tucked it in her bag.

Moved by her hysterical cries, I ran for my puncture kit and made a hasty repair. After much huffing and puffing at the pump, Henry was restored to his full glory. But I would not easily forget the look of intense hatred my wife aimed at me then. She jumped into the car, slammed the door and drove away with Henry, tyres screeching.

The following Saturday, I woke up with a raging toothache. 'I suppose I'd better take you to the dentist,' my wife said. She was clearly irritated by my moans and groans. 'I'm going to the hairdresser. You can sort yourself out while I have my roots touched up.'

She insisted that Henry come along with us. 'We can't leave the car in those back streets without someone to look after it. There's plenty of room in the back if you keep your knees tucked up.'

An icy wind was blowing as I staggered to the dentist. He fixed me up with a temporary filling, but it was still very painful. I arrived back at the car in an awful mood. My wife was not yet there, but Henry still sat, smiling, in the front seat. The sight of him was too much for me.

I opened the door and dragged him out by the arm. I had seen a large rubbish skip nearby. As I relaxed my grip for a moment, a mighty gust of wind seized him. His posh cap fell off into the gutter. Up and away went Henry, flying out of sight over the rooftops. I gazed up after him, then chuckled, 'Good riddance!' My wife would think that he had been stolen.

I decided to wander round for a bit. I didn't want to be there when she discovered that he was missing. I smirked to myself. She was crazy about Henry. She would kill me if she knew what I had done.

As I rounded the corner, I could see

something happening further down the street. Feeling curious, I walked towards the town square, and what a scene I found there! Blue lights flashed from police cars and ambulances. Everyone was gazing up at the church tower. There, on the edge, was a human form. I knew it at once by the tartan scarf which attached it to the stone. It was Henry.

A policeman was speaking to him through a loudhailer. 'Now come along, sir, just make your way back down the stairs. My officers are there to help you.'

The crowd groaned as Henry swayed in the breeze.

I pushed forward. 'Officer, officer . . .!' But I was silenced by angry murmurs from the crowd.

They all moaned as a gust of wind freed Henry and he teetered on the edge. I could hear myself moaning, too. Not from fear, but from an agonizing pain between my shoulder blades. It felt as though a sharp skewer was being driven into my body. As I twisted round, I saw my wife disappear into the crowd. No one else noticed her. All eyes were fixed on the drama above us.

As my knees began to buckle I saw Henry float gently by. He had a triumphant smile upon his lips.

THE LOST GENE

Angela Coughlan

I always see things in black and white. No shades of grey ever cloud my view of events. I tend to tell it like it is, 'call a spade a spade', so to speak.

That's not to say I think that's the way it should be for everyone. But it's how I see things.

My mother, however, saw life through those famous rose-coloured glasses. No matter how serious a problem or unlikeable a person was, Mother always saw some good in it or them. The pot was always half full for her, never half empty. She was always an optimist.

I have never understood whether or not such optimism is a gift one is born with, or a disadvantage one passes on. Perhaps that is the one question I should have asked her.

'Horses for courses,' she would probably have replied. Or perhaps, *'Carpe diem'*. Seize the day.

She was fond of such sayings. As a child I remember being fascinated by them, thinking her highly intelligent.

Even when it rained, Mother would still take us to the seaside. The moats of our sandcastles often filled up with rainwater rather than the flowing tide.

'Come on, children,' she'd say. 'Eat your sandwiches before they get too wet.'

Not even the rain could dampen her smile. Hard-boiled eggs were sometimes runny like our noses. To Mum that was all part of the fun.

Even now I can picture her under her umbrella, paddling at the water's edge. She'd tuck her skirt into her waistband while we bathed, jumped up and down and splashed her.

When I think about it now, it's a wonder we didn't all catch cold. It occurs to me that I haven't done anything like that with my daughters. I wouldn't have the patience, or perhaps the courage. And can you believe it? Mum once took us to the Zoo, knowing it was closed. She said there was a small chance we might see some of the animals over the wall. It's true, I swear it. Amazingly we did see, for one short moment, a giraffe's head. Actually, it was Mum who said she saw it.

Where, I wonder, did that gene go? How come I didn't inherit it?

When I think back to my schooldays, I was never picked for the school plays. Mum said it was because they needed a good clapper like me in the audience. I believed her.

Other mothers were active in the PTA. They'd go to regular school meetings or run around like headless chickens on sports day. They would forever discuss extra teaching for their kids. My mother was busy at home making fairy cakes and lemonade, lost in daydreams about me saving the world from a rare disease. I was eleven when I became aware Mum was an eccentric. One day I heard the other mothers call her that. I didn't know what it meant but eccentric became a beautiful word to me.

Mum was Mum. As children we wouldn't have changed her for the world. Sometimes we were bored and made too much noise around the house. Mum would tell us to watch telly then.

'There's nothing on!' we'd shout.

'Yes, there is!' she'd shout back, turning the TV on. 'Look at those pretty colours.'

The amazing thing is, we would believe her and we'd sit and watch the test card.

Again I ask myself, where did that gene go? How come I didn't inherit it?

At seventeen my mother had become pregnant with me. Over the years, I never once heard her speak any words of regret or complaint that her teenage years were taken from her. At twenty Mum had married my stepdad and had two more children. Dad, as I knew him, also had a very optimistic outlook on life. They were well suited. When they did fight, it was over issues that we, as children, thought were funny.

'If things don't change they'll have to stay as they are,' she'd say.

'As things improve so they'll get better,' he'd answer.

And we'd all laugh.

It's said that most young people go through a stage of being embarrassed by their parents. They avoid bringing their friends home. For me it was the opposite. My friends loved my crazy mother and loved to stop over. To Mum, music was meant to be played loud, carpets were designed to soak up spilt cola. There was no such thing as bedtime.

I just loved our 'girly chats', as she called them.

'What was your first thought, Mum, when you realized you were expecting me?' I once asked.

I was expecting her to tell me of her fears. Of the shame of being an unmarried mum in those days.

'Oh!' she replied, with a thrill in her voice. 'I hoped it would be a girl – and I couldn't wait for you to grow up and be a doctor.'

'I must be a disappointment to you then, Mum,' I replied, looking at my shop assistant's uniform.

'Disappointment? Never!'

Then, as if donning her rose-tinted glasses, she added something.

'If the good Lord had wanted you to be a doctor, he'd have made you one.'

Had she really meant that? Or was it her eccentric way of hiding her disappointment? That, alas, is something I'll never know.

Sadly Mum has been gone quite a few years now. When the end was near, it was she who held my hand – not I hers.

If she could have granted me one last wish, I'd like to have known what happened to that gene.

I find myself thinking of her today because my daughter rang last night. She says she's coming home this weekend from medical school. 'If it rains, can we take Gran's ashes to the seaside?' she asked. I'm very proud of her, and my mother was too.

THERE'S A QUEUE FOR THE THERAPIST'S CHAIR

Colette Dickinson

THERE'S A QUEUE FOR the therapist's chair. I should know – it's my chair. Charles arrives while I'm massaging Mrs Turnbull's feet, and behind him is Lily. She's a dear and hovers sweetly. I ask Charles to wait but he's as grumpy as ever. Reflexology can't be rushed. I need to concentrate. I push my thumb along the ball of Mrs Turnbull's foot. It reveals what is going on in her entire body.

'Your digestion's a bit spongy today,' I tell her. 'Are you still avoiding wheat?'

'Well, no, Jane,' she says, lifting her head a little to watch my hands. 'I only gave it up for a week. Now I'm cutting out carbohydrates. The trouble is, all I've got in my cupboards is carbs.'

'Mmmm.' I try to listen to her but I can hear Charles moaning about time and a key.

It is amazing how busy I've been lately – and how very unexpected. Drives me nuts sometimes. I barely have time to think.

'Would you like ten minutes of reiki healing to finish off?' I ask Mrs Turnbull.

'Oooh, yes, please.' Mrs Turnbull wriggles into the pillows. 'Tell me what reiki is again, Jane?'

'Well . . .' I place the blanket over Mrs Turnbull's belly, smoothing it across her pleated skirt and mohair cardigan. 'Imagine I'm like a television aerial, channelling energy into you. It can heal any parts of your body that are sore. It takes away negative energy.'

'Oh, yes, I was trying to tell my Bill about it. He thinks it's a load of rubbish.'

'Fair enough,' I say. 'That's what my Tom thought at first.'

Poor Tom. He must wonder what he married sometimes. I was a shop assistant when we first got together. Thanks to his support, I'm now doing this. Yet he was a real doubting Thomas in the beginning until I got hold of his feet.

'So my smelly size elevens are a map of my whole body, are they?' He was doubtful even

26

after I'd explained reflexology to him. 'Well, the only person who will ever touch my feet will be the undertaker,' he declared then. Now he can't get enough of it!

He's a real convert – even to reiki. It was his Great-Aunt Beryl who swung it for him. She came one day and gave him a piece of her mind. Told him to stop being so cynical and to believe what he was seeing and feeling. It freaked him out a bit, but Tom said she always did. A very strong character, Beryl. I'd realized that for myself.

Mrs Turnbull lies back and closes her eyes. I close mine, completely focused now. I place my hands above her abdomen and there's a hot, fizzing feeling – almost like electricity coming off her. I move my hands up towards her head. Suddenly I feel dizzy and a sharp pain stings my left ear.

'Had any trouble with your ears, Mrs Turnbull?'

'Oh, yes, dear. Awful earache keeps coming and going in the left one.'

Thankfully the dizziness subsides. As it does, Charles starts up again.

'Tell her I'm waiting!' he shouts. My hackles

rise. Does he have no manners? I almost yell at him to go away, but that wouldn't do much for my aura of peace and serenity.

I take a deep breath. Mrs Turnbull's hour is nearly up. I could cut it short now, I suppose. But I just can't bring myself to do so.

'Mrs Turnbull?'

'Yes, Jane.'

'Charles is here. He says he's waiting.'

'Not him again. I told you . . .'

Charles interrupts.

'I can't wait all day, you know. You never gave me your answer last time.'

'He is mad about you, isn't he, Mrs Turnbull? That was so lovely of him, proposing to you by the river that day.'

'Yes, but it was a long time ago. I'm twenty years married now. Why won't he go away?'

'I'm not very good at sending people away. He's my client, like all the others.'

'So am I!' Mrs Turnbull's dark blue eyes open suddenly. 'Honestly, Jane – I just came here for some therapy. Not to be hounded by an ex-boyfriend!'

'I know, Mrs Turnbull. I'm sorry. It is strange he's so insistent. That's love, I guess.'

28

'Love? Hmph! He was after my money.' Mrs Turnbull folds her arms under her bosom. 'He knew I inherited my father's fortune when I reached twenty-one. "You've got the key to the door," he said to me on my birthday. "Yes, and you're not having it!" I told him.'

Charles has gone quiet so I assume he has heard this. I sigh. No, this really was not what I had in mind when I became a therapist.

So many clients need to offload. Some need comfort. Some are lonely, I think, and just want some contact. Some just love a chat.

There are the others, of course – with back problems, migraines, strains and low energy levels. Some of them have massage, some have reiki, some have reflexology. Some have a bit of all three! Yes, I'm very flexible. But relation-ship guidance? Now that was not in my training. Still, it's all part of the service. It was when I began to practise reiki that it all really took off.

'When did Charles die?' I ask Mrs Turnbull as she pays me.

'I'm not sure, love. We lost touch when I married.'

I help her to put her coat on.

'Doesn't it scare you, Jane? All these voices from the Other Side in your head?'

'Not really. Doing reiki seemed to open up some spiritual channel in me. They drive me nuts sometimes, but I just tell them to leave me alone. It does freak Tom out a bit – especially when his Great-Aunt Beryl comes through.'

I pause, focusing my mind back to the open door within.

'Your Granny Lily is here too today, but Charles won't let her get a word in. Did she have a maroon handbag with a gold clasp?'

'Yes!' says Mrs Turnbull.

'I think she's just clouted him with it.'

Mrs Turnbull potters away smiling, her digestive system flowing smoothly.

There's a queue for the therapist's chair, but for now the door is closed.

I DON'T KNOW WHY

Terence Foster

Dave

I DON'T KNOW WHY he does it, my boss. I haven't got a clue. But he's wrecking my life. I'm telling you, from day one he's had it in for me. Day *one*. Whatever I say, whatever I do, it's not good enough. I haven't done anything to him. I just keep my head down and work hard.

What makes it worse is, there's *nothing* I can do about it. I mean, I've got a family to support, you know? A wife and a beautiful son. He's only twelve years old, our boy Billy, a growing lad. Relies on me to put food on the table for him. And I'm going to buy him some football boots, the best that money can buy. Nike Air Legends.

I'm putting money aside for him, working extra shifts. I want him to have an education, you see, a future. I don't want him ending up in a factory like me, he's too good for that. Don't want him stacking crates and lifting boxes. Taking orders from some muppet like his old man has to. You'd love him if you saw him – a little blond lad he is but strong for his age. Loves his football more than anything in the whole world. He's a little hero, my son. Everybody says so.

Missed his Cup Final to take on a weekend shift at work, didn't I? Gutted I was. But I had to work. Would have been more trouble than it was worth to try and say no. It would just have given the boss another excuse to pick a fight or take away my extra shifts when I really needed them. I don't want to give him any excuses to do anything. Old Billy still scored the winner even without his old man – a left-foot volley in the second half of extra time. Told me all about it he did. I was pleased as Punch.

There's nothing I can do about work. I've got a family to feed, and that's that. Some things you just have to live with.

Linda
I don't know why he does it. I really don't. Things never used to be like this. Dave used to be kind and gentle. Used to act like he loved

me. Now he's only got time for his son, although not nearly enough. Didn't even go to watch his Cup Final on Saturday, the biggest game of Billy's life. Dave's either working or sleeping these days. Or sometimes he just sits there and stares into space. I don't know what's wrong with him. He won't even talk to me any more, let alone open up. Sometimes I lie awake crying, right next to him, my heart breaking. And he doesn't even move.

And as for the bruises, well, I'm running out of excuses. That's three he's given me this year, and it's only March. I used the one about walking into a door. That seemed to work okay. Then I had one on my arm and I thought I'd got away with it, with my long-sleeved jumper on. But I rolled my sleeves up at the tenpin bowling alley, without thinking, and they all saw. Told the girls I did it gardening. Think they believed me. And the third one . . . well, I haven't left the house since he gave it to me. I'm still thinking about it. I'm sure I'll come up with something.

Don't get me wrong, mind you. He's not normally like this. He must just be going through a rough patch at the moment. You know, like people do. Everyone has rough patches.

Billy

I don't know why she does it. She yells at me all the time, and sometimes she just ignores me. I do my homework, I tidy my room, and I eat my dinner, even when there are things in it that are horrible, like runner beans, peas and sprouts. I always say thank you when I get a lift to football. I try to behave, because I know my mum is unhappy. I don't mean to get in the way.

When I grow up, I want to be a footballer. Wayne Rooney is my favourite player, even though I support Liverpool. But it's okay that Wayne is my favourite player because he plays for England as well. I support them too because that's my country. That's allowed, dad says. I'm a striker, the same as Wayne. I want to be just like him when I grow up. I will work hard for the team and score goals and be the fans' favourite. Hopefully, when I play well they will chant my name and sing songs about me.

Dad comes to most of my games. But he missed my Cup Final, which I was gutted about. I told my mum and dad a white lie about that match. Because neither of them came it was easy. I told them I scored the winning goal, in the top corner of the net. With my left foot. Which is extra good because I'm right-footed.

I think they believed me, which is lucky. I don't want them to know what really happened. See, what really happened is, I got a red card. A straight red. Like David Beckham got against Argentina in the World Cup when I was only five. I know about it because I remember dad screaming and swearing at the television. He wanted to *kill* Beckham for getting sent off. I'm worried dad might be angry with me too if he finds out.

Anyway, what happened was that one of the other team laughed at my Hi-Tecs. He said I could never afford decent boots because my dad works in a warehouse. So I got upset and hit him. As hard as I could. And I smashed his nose, and there was blood everywhere, all over his shirt. It was the first red card of my career.

I wish my dad could have been there.

I don't know why he wasn't.

LAST GASP

Richard Grant

IT WAS DARK WHEN Brooke Aston rode her
scooter into the cul-de-sac where her grandfather lived. Suburbia was kept at bay by a high
security fence. Inside stood a number of
warden-controlled bungalows. The metal-link
fence made them look more like cell blocks in
an open prison.

She parked the scooter on a patch of tarmac
reserved for the residents of Blackheath Senior
Homes. Her two-year-old silver Vespa looked
out of place there. Brooke stood staring at the
tall, lime-green-painted gate to the sheltered
housing. After taking off her helmet, she lit a
cigarette. She seemed to inhale everything that
was wrong with the world and let it grow inside
her lungs. It felt oddly comforting.

Using the key her grandfather had given her,
Brooke opened the gate and went straight to his
house.

'Who's there?' called a distant voice. 'Brooke?'

She put the cigarette out on the sole of her shoe, saving the stub. 'Yeah, it's me.'

She walked into the bungalow. Most of the lights were out and the rooms were dark and gloomy. Her grandfather sat in brooding silence in his armchair. No TV or radio chatter to break the mood.

'You're an hour late,' he said in a faint, out-of-character voice. Eighty-two he may have been, but he had never seemed old until now.

'Sorry,' said Brooke. 'Had second thoughts.'

Coughing in deep discomfort, her grand-father got shakily to his feet. 'You're a good girl, Brooky, I never doubted that you'd come.'

'Granddad . . .'

'We're late. Need to go.'

Brooke nodded. She helped her grandfather get his coat on then led him out of the bungalow. She took care to lock both door and gate as they went.

It was not easy getting him on to the Vespa. He was frail and had no sense of balance. Once he was steady on the back Brooke was able to secure his old army rucksack. Gently she eased her spare helmet over his grey head.

'Okay,' she said, with a wry grin, 'you look ready to rumble.'

'Let's roll,' he announced, waving one fist in the air.

Chuckling to herself, Brooke mounted the Vespa and put on her own helmet. She turned the key in the ignition. The little engine coughed into life. With a nudge of the kick-stand and a turn of the throttle they were off. They rode in silence for much of the way. It was close to midnight on a weekday and the roads were empty. Thirteen miles from Blackheath, through West Bromwich and on towards Witton. The night air was chilly.

At some traffic lights Brooke turned and looked back at her grandfather, as best she could.

'Mum's asked me to move out,' she said bitterly.

The lights turned green. It did not take long for them to reach their destination, the main gates to Witton Cemetery.

After helping him off the scooter, Brooke picked up her grandfather's bag. She led him to the tall gates. Thanks to a friend who worked there, she had a key to open them.

They walked silently for a minute or two, following the weak glow of her small torch. Grandfather spoke first.

'All right, what did you say to your mother?'

Brooke was glad she could not see the look on his face.

'Nothing new.'

'Well, there's your problem, young lady. You can only call someone a bitch so many times before they snap.'

Brooke had never heard him say a word like that before. It came as quite a shock.

They left the narrow concrete path and wandered over grassy rises lined with graves. Overhead hung dark tangled shapes which could be recognized as trees in the daylight. Taking the torch from Brooke, her grandfather walked over to one of the graves. He shone the beam on its headstone. Brooke stayed where she was. This looked like a private moment, one she did not need to disturb.

The moment lasted long enough for one drag on a new cigarette.

'Come here, Brooky,' said her grandfather.

She dropped the cigarette and went over to him.

'Show me your arms,' he said.

Taken aback, she said, 'What?'

'Please.'

A long silent moment passed as she stared at his serious face. Then, slowly, Brooke rolled up one of her sleeves. Her grandfather shone the torch on twenty or so narrow cuts which ran all the way down her arm.

'Oh, Brooky,' he said sadly.

'How did you know?' she asked, shocked and upset.

Her grandfather shone the light back on the headstone. The name on it read 'Hans Gurbach'.

'At midnight Mr Gurbach will have been dead exactly sixty-six years,' he said.

Brooke stared at the grave, not sure what he meant.

'Sixty-six years exactly since I ended his life by shooting him in the back.'

She gasped.

'He was an escaped prisoner,' her grandfather said. 'I was very young and in the Home Guard. I was told they were armed . . . it was dark, like this . . . all excuses really.'

She didn't know what to say. Her grandfather shone the light back on her arm.

'I'm old, Brooky. Not much time left. So listen to me, OK?' he said earnestly. 'Life is important. While you're lucky enough to have no shadow hanging over you, you must live it, not hate it.'

Brooke rolled her sleeve back down.

'There's a tent in the bag,' he said. 'We're going to see the morning in with Mr Gurbach. Keep him company for a while.'

MURDER IN CATCHER'S WOOD

Paul Horsman

SIMON KNEW HE SHOULDN'T be using Catcher's Wood as a short cut.

Not since the murder . . .

Her name was Miss Phelps. She'd taught at Simon's school. Had done for almost two years. Information Technology had been her subject. She'd been made head of the IT department only a month before it had happened.

Strangled, the police report had said. Strangled by some type of cord and a strong pair of hands.

But who would want to kill such a promising young teacher? That was the question which was still on everybody's lips. Because the killer had not yet been caught. And there appeared to be no one at all who might have wanted Miss Phelps dead. Family, friends and co-workers couldn't speak more highly of her. Even her students sang her praises. The woman had no enemies, it appeared.

Simon had to admit he was nervous. Only two months had passed since Miss Phelps's lifeless body had been discovered in Catcher's Wood in a clearing, not too far from where he now hurried. Maybe it was too soon . . .

But he was late for school. The second time this week. And cutting through Catcher's Wood would shave five minutes off his journey.

Though there was another reason for Simon's cutting through the wood. He'd come to collect something. Something he'd left here a few months back. Something which would land him in a lot of trouble if anyone discovered it.

Simon found the tree. This was definitely the one. He'd fixed it in his mind, used a nearby stump as a reference point.

He went behind the tree and reached up. There was a small hollow, from which he pulled something silver and square. A digital camera.

The name of his school was etched on its underside.

He removed something else from the hollow, too. A computer cable. Quickly he dropped both items into his satchel. Then glanced around, anxiously.

What if . . .

But everybody believed Miss Phelps's killer to be long gone. Why would they return to the scene of the crime? So Simon relaxed a little. Still, the sooner he was out of Catcher's Wood the better.

Where was Mr Lewis?

Mr Vickers, the head teacher, could hear Class 3L – Simon's class – from the other end of the corridor. It was enough to give him a headache. And he already had a headache.

Then Mr Lewis appeared. Hurrying down the corridor. Out of breath. Wearing an apologetic smile. This wasn't the first time he'd arrived late over these last few weeks. But Vickers supposed he could overlook it once more.

Lewis was a long-serving and dedicated member of staff. And it couldn't have been easy for him, replacing the late Miss Phelps as head of IT.

Simon left a rather rushed roll-call and went to his first lesson of the day. But he couldn't concentrate. On that lesson or any other. His thoughts were only on the camera. He had to know, had to check.

Which was why, at half-past three that afternoon, while most of the school was heading towards the school gates, he climbed the stairs to the IT room. He didn't feel too out of place, though. He often used to stay behind after school to work in the IT room.

Simon approached the doors. On one of them was a brass sign.

It used to read: *Head of IT – Miss V. Phelps.*

Now it read: *Head of IT – Mr S. Lewis.*

Simon pushed through the doors. Thankfully everybody had left. He sat down at one of the laptops at the far end of the room. Next he took some files from his satchel so it would look as though he was working. Then he removed the camera and USB cable, which he connected to the laptop. The camera was very basic. It had no LCD screen to show the pictures stored in its memory.

A few clicks later and Simon was viewing the stored images. Numerous pictures of different trees. A series of shots, blurred and indistinct. Then a shot of a hand, gripping something.

Finally, a face . . . a face twisted with hatred.

So Miss Phelps *had* got a picture of her killer.

Simon smiled as he deleted the images from both the camera and the laptop.

Nobody would find him out now.

He'd *had* to kill her, you see. She'd stolen his job. *Her*, with her youthful ideas and her fancy computer degree! She had barely been here five minutes! The head of IT post should have been his from the start. Twenty years' loyal service he'd given this school.

It had been quite easy really. Following Miss Phelps into Catcher's Wood that afternoon. Sneaking up behind her. They'd even had a friendly chat before that, when she'd come to borrow the camera from the IT room. Something about getting some shots for a nature studies web page she and her students were working on.

Simon had scolded himself later for leaving that camera and cable in the wood. But he'd panicked. Had thought he'd heard somebody coming and he hadn't wanted to be caught with the camera. He had hidden the incriminating evidence and then he had run.

He'd felt sure the police would find it. They'd scoured the wood for weeks.

Only now did he dare risk returning for the evidence. And it was a risk. What if somebody saw him so close to the crime scene . . . saw him remove the camera . . . thought it strange he should be in the wood at all?

But they hadn't.

And all that was left now was to dispose of the camera.

Though he was going to *hang* on to this. Simon wrapped the USB cable around both hands and pulled it taut, so it cracked like a whip.

You see, *Simon Lewis, head of IT* had a nice ring to it.

But *Simon Lewis, head teacher* sounded even better.

And, well, who knew? Old Vickers might soon be taking early retirement . . .

CHRISTMAS TRUCE

Jeanette Middlemas

THERE WAS NO DOUBT about it, our dad was a bit of a drunk.

'He's been in the pub again,' mam would say. 'Best keep out of his way.'

And we did. We learned early on you don't argue with a drunk.

Mam could drink as well, mind you. Not every night like him, but when they'd both been drinking, the fights were spectacular. It wasn't backchat which filled most of their days, but real fireworks. I'd lie awake listening, not really knowing what they were saying, hearing muffled shouts and threats. Mam's voice was always the loudest.

My Auntie Alice had a lot to say about dad.

'I'd rather eat coal than live with a man like that,' she'd say.

'You want to try eating coal, and feeding it to your kids,' mam would reply.

That was their excuse. That they stayed together for us. But even then I knew it was daft. They just loved hating each other. Years later, when they did split up, mam cried for three days. I could never figure it out.

When dad was sober, he was fine. He was Irish, and had the gift of the gab. He'd got those Irish looks and laughing eyes, a bit like Georgie Best. He was especially nice to me sometimes. When he was, I loved him to bits.

'Apple of his eye, she is,' mam would say. 'Pity he can't be as nice to me!'

So I felt guilty for loving my dad. You couldn't love both of them, you had to take sides.

Dad loved reading. There were always lots of books in the house. He introduced me and my brother to them when we were young. He got us to go to the local library and we were hooked. We read everything. The schools in our area were a joke. If it hadn't been for dad we'd barely have been able to read or write.

I've always loved Christmas although I'm never sure why, since it was always a good excuse for some firecracker fights between mam and dad. One Christmas when I was eight and my brother five I lay awake, reading my book. I knew I had some time before they came back from the pub. My little brother was fast asleep. The booze flowed freely, of course, at Christmas. They both came home drunk as skunks. The row had started early on when dad had taken a shine to one of the barmaids. He never had any trouble attracting the girls.

I heard mam trying to goad him into feeling as angry as she was. 'I've always fancied your Tony, you know,' she announced. Tony was his younger and more handsome brother. It worked. Dad flew into a rage. He called her a whore, and a lot of other names I'd never heard before.

The only reason I was still awake was because it was Christmas Eve. I'd wanted to know if Santa would come. Heaven knows what he would have made of those two if he had come down our chimney. The upshot of it was that dad went to bed, locking her out of the bedroom. I lay there shaking. My brother was deep in sleep. I could hear mam banging on their bedroom door. The presents were in there and it was nearly Christmas Day.

She was yelling about not being able to give

her children a good Christmas. It was all his fault, of course. Why she thought our Christmas would be magical because of a few gifts, I don't know. After a bit mam went back downstairs. She probably fell asleep on the settee. All was quiet.

I couldn't sleep after all this excitement. After a while I put the light on so I could finish my book. I must have been reading for about an hour, lost in the story, when suddenly I looked up. Dad was on the landing, looking at me. I hadn't heard him open the door, I was so deep into my book. He was just standing there, looking at me. Guiltily I put my book away. I thought he was going to shout at me for reading when I should have been asleep. But he didn't. He had a really strange look on his face. He seemed to have been struck dumb. He went and brought all the Christmas presents from the bedroom. He stacked them at the top of the stairs and then went back to bed.

Next morning mam started to cook the turkey, and then to peel potatoes. We had opened our presents and were playing with them by the fire. It was cold outside. Dad didn't get up until midday. They totally ignored each other. We all sat down to Christmas dinner in silence. Mam dished up, and we started to eat. No one had the heart to pull the Christmas crackers.

Dad suddenly stopped eating. He put his knife and fork down and bowed his head over his plate. To my amazement, I saw he was crying. I'd never seen my dad cry.

'I'm sorry,' he sobbed.

Mam rushed over to him and put her arms round him. 'It's all right,' she said. 'I'm sorry too!' And they looked a proper picture, her cradling his head in her arms.

What a relief! We went on to enjoy that meal, and there was real laughter and fun that day. Fortunately, the pubs didn't open on Christmas Day, so there wasn't one argument.

Perhaps that's why I like Christmas. It's a time of truce.

Like those troops in the First World War. You know the story? About how they stopped fighting on Christmas Day, the Brits and the Germans. They had a football match instead, before they went back to knocking hell out of each other. Because that's exactly what mam and dad did. As soon as that blissful day was

over they went back to their normal arguing.
And we couldn't wait for the next Christmas
Day.

DAD'S CAR

Stuart Real

DAD'S CAR WAS BLUE. Actually it used to be blue. Now only small patches of blue paint could be seen between the mud, dirt and rust. That was the outside. The inside was worse. Every surface was covered in dust. The door pockets had hundreds of empty crisp packets shoved into them. The packets that were not pushed in deeply enough were on the floor. There was rubbish all over it too, empty carrier bags, sweet wrappers and bits of grass.

Kyle sat in the back of dad's car. He was travelling home from school. His brother Zak sat in the front seat next to dad. Kyle liked travelling in his dad's car because he was allowed to eat and drink there. It didn't matter if he accidentally spilt anything. Mum would never allow eating in her car as it might make a mess.

The radio was playing very loudly and Kyle

was eating sausage and chips. They were perched on his lap in their paper. He couldn't hear what his dad and brother were talking about because the music was far too loud. He looked out of the window as he munched his food.

'Can I have one?' he heard a voice say. He looked at the seat next to him. Sitting by the other window was a small green man. He had pointy ears, huge yellow eyes and a big smile.

'Pardon?'

'I said, can I have one?'

'One what?' asked Kyle.

'One of your chips. It would be nice to have a hot one instead of the cold ones I find on the floor. They are usually covered in fluff.'

The little man reached his hand over to Kyle's chip paper. Kyle slapped it away. 'Oi! They're mine.'

'Oh, go on,' said the green man. 'You never eat all of them anyway.'

'How do you know that?'

'Because I live here. I've seen you.'

'Where do you live?' asked Kyle.

'Here in your dad's car,' replied the little man. 'I live behind the back seat, in the boot.'

56

Kyle handed him a chip. 'What's your name?' he asked.

The little man snatched the chip from Kyle's hand and stuffed it into his mouth. He blew air from his mouth a few times and waved at it with his hand. 'That's a bit hot,' he mumbled. 'My name is Zinzan.'

'Why are you in my dad's car, Zinzan?' asked Kyle, handing the little chap another chip.

Zinzan blew on the chip then shoved it whole into his mouth. 'I live here. Well, I don't actually live *here*, I live in the boot.'

'Why?'

'I'm a rubbish sprite,' answered Zinzan, holding out his hand for another chip. 'My job is to tidy up the rubbish people leave behind.'

'So, do you just tidy up and then leave?'

'Usually, but this car is a bit much to tidy in one go. I've been here nearly seven months now. I had only just finished the boot before it got messy again. I've got a feeling I could be here a long while.'

Zinzan suddenly screamed and held his hands over his pointy ears. He closed his eyes so tightly that his face screwed up too.

57

Kyle looked around the car and could not see what was scaring the rubbish sprite. He looked out of the window and under the seats too. There was nothing else for it. He gently peeled Zinzan's long fingers away from his left ear and whispered to him.

'What's wrong? Are you OK?'

'It's that noise, that horrible noise!'

'What noise?' Kyle asked, listening very hard.

'The noise the one you call dad makes. Is someone trying to hurt him? He sounds wounded.'

Kyle laughed and gave Zinzan another chip. 'He's not hurt, he's just singing. He's happy.'

'That's singing? It's *horrible*. How do you cope with it?'

'You get used to it after a while.'

For the rest of the journey home Kyle and Zinzan shared Kyle's chips. They played a whole host of games, from I spy to See Who Can Find the Most Cars of Their Chosen Colour. Dad continued to 'screech'. Every now and then Zinzan would shield his ears with his hands. Finally the car pulled up outside their home. 'We're back,' dad said, giving Zak a gentle nudge to wake him up. Dad turned round to wake Kyle too because he always fell asleep on long journeys.

Kyle just sat there, smiling, and said, 'I know.'

'What shall we do with our chip papers, Dad?' asked Zak in a sleepy voice.

'Just leave them there. I'll clear them up later.'

Kyle left his chip paper on the back seat and winked at Zinzan. He was hiding under dad's seat. Zinzan smiled back at his friend and extended a long hand to grab some cold chips.

After the weekend, dad was loading the boys' bags into the boot of the car. 'Whose turn is it to sit in the front this time?' he sighed. There was always an argument over who could sit in the front and who had to sit in the back.

'Zak's!' shouted Kyle excitedly, climbing into the back.

'But I thought it was your turn,' said dad.

'It is, but I enjoy it in the back.'

Kyle pulled on his seatbelt and looked down under dad's seat. He could see two yellow eyes blinking up at him. Zinzan already had his hands over his ears.

'Dad?'

'Yes, Kyle?'

'Please don't sing this time.'

THE SUN BOOK OF SHORT STORIES

SUPER

Michael Ripley

SAM COVERED HIS FACE with his hands. He had to protect himself from the shards of glass flying his way. He felt the sharp edges digging into the backs of his arms. They stung his ears and the other parts of his face he couldn't cover.

But he had forgotten to brace himself against the shock wave that followed. The sound filled his ears, making him think his head was going to explode. It felt like a melon hitting the ground from five storeys. He staggered back but kept his footing. Half a billion pieces of glass whooshed past his head at the speed of sound.

With his ears still ringing, he shook his face and forearms so the splinters flew off. He dusted the tiny specks from his brow while scanning the sky for his foe. Julian was still where he had been before unleashing the explosion. His legs were spread, knees bent, head bowed and arms flexed in front of him. Sam could see he was trying to recoup the energy spent on his last move. He had to act fast.

He tilted his head back and closed his eyes, summoning his power. Slowly, he brought his right hand, clenched in a fist, to the side of his head. As he felt the energy coursing through his veins, his hand began to glow bright white. When the glow became brilliant, he brought his fist down on the ground with a ten-megaton force.

The instant his hand made contact, the earth shattered around it. Lumps of soil and clay flew up into the air around him. A jagged crack shot out from the impact crater, straight towards Julian. Before he could fully recover he was thrown off balance by the shearing earth beneath him. Sam decided to follow up quickly. He took off like a lightning bolt, leaving a faded imprint of himself and a faint blue trail.

Fast as a bullet, he reached Julian just as he was getting to his feet. He barely had time to brace himself for Sam's cosmic shoulder charge. Julian flew backwards through the air, straight through the wall of a nearby house. It instantly collapsed on top of him.

Sam stood there on the scarred battlefield.

His chest was heaving, his head raised to the sky seeking cleaner air. The follow-up move had drained him of strength. It would take him a while to recharge after this. But the combat wasn't over yet. As the last grains of dust were falling on the wrecked house, rubble at the top of the pile started to shudder and shake violently.

A green streak escaped from the top. Julian flew hundreds of feet into the air. He came to a rest, hovering above the ground, head back and arms and legs spread. He clenched his fists so that his biceps bulged and looked as though they might pop. Sam could see he was drawing energy directly from the sun.

A pure yellow ray shot from the upper atmosphere and engulfed Julian in a glowing ball of power. He unleashed the energy at once, directed as a wide beam towards the ground. It landed just by Sam. Guided by Julian's hands, it quickly swept across the earth towards him. Caught in the intense shaft of light, Sam could feel every drop of water in his body boil. The attack was short-lived but ferocious. He crumpled and withered, steam rising from his burnt skin.

Still using the sun's energy, Julian followed up this attack with an even faster one. He turned in mid-air and propelled himself forward at the speed of light. Sam lay helpless on the ground below.

The impact threw lumps of rock and clouds of dust far and wide. It gathered at its highest point and rolled back over itself in a mushroom shape. The whole earth shook. The sound formed a solid barrier, crumbling anything still standing.

The sound faded to a rippling murmur and the dust coated everything in a grey-brown layer. Sam slowly opened his eyes. His whole body was numb and broken. He was lying at the bottom of a deep crater. Julian sat on his chest, fist raised above his head. He realized there was still life left in his crushed enemy. The whole forearm attached to the raised fist began slowly to rotate. It picked up speed, spinning faster and faster until it was just a blur.

He was about to drill Sam's now fragile skull into the ground. Then a sound louder than any of their battle had created boomed across the planet. It shook the very sky. Clods of earth broke loose from the walls of the crater and came tumbling down.

'Dinner's ready, boys!' it bellowed. 'Come and wash your hands.'

Julian pulled Sam to his feet. Immediately both boys turned into Harrier jump jets. Their vertical take-off jets kicked in, keeping them in position while they turned towards the sound. The engines fired, thrusting both planes forward, accelerating quickly to Mach 1.

Keeping low to the ground, beneath radar detection, the two planes weaved in and out of each other's paths. The lead plane veered suddenly in front of the other and then slowed, allowing it to pass.

'I'll take the starboard approach,' Sam said into his hand.

'Roger that,' replied Julian. He removed his hand from the plane's controls and clasped it over his own mouth. 'I'll come in high.'

The two planes began their final approach up the garden path in perfect formation. Their mother ruffled each boy's hair as they ducked beneath her arm and through the open door.

'Hope you two have been playing nicely,' she said.

SHE

Daniel Rowe

I OPEN MY EYES. The late-afternoon sun momentarily blinds me. Where am I? I look around. Fields. All I can see is fields. Well, there are a few hills in the distance, and the odd farmhouse every now and again. But mostly it's just fields. I could be anywhere in England. I look at my watch, or where my watch used to be. I wish I hadn't given it back to Rachel. Damn pride.

'Good morning, sleepy.'

I turn around to see what annoyingly cheerful person is sitting next to me now. I hate trains.

I'm greeted by a smile that could warm the coldest of hearts. Why is she so happy?

'Hi,' she chirps. Rachel has the same top as the one this girl is wearing.

'Hi,' I reply.

I look back out of the window. Another farmhouse passes by, and some more fields.

'Don't you find it weird, the way two people can sit next to each other without saying anything?'

'I haven't really thought about it,' I murmur.

'What's your name?' she asks me.

'Luke,' I answer, as I turn back round to face her. She's still smiling. For the first time, though, I realize that she is quite pretty. An exotic, strangely familiar face, with deep brown eyes, and topped with long, dark hair. Probably could've been a model. Might even *be* a model, she seems to have the body of one. Well, as best as I can tell. She is sitting down.

'What's your name?' I ask.

'I'm—' she starts to reply, before being drowned out. Another train is rumbling past in the other direction.

'I'm sorry, I didn't quite catch that!' I shout over the racket.

'I'm—'

Damn! Missed it again. Not that it's important.

'Please to meet you,' I say, smiling politely.

She laughs. I have no idea why.

'Where are you from?' I ask, not really interested.

'Doesn't matter,' she replies. 'What sort of music do you like?'

'Excuse me?'

'Music. You know – songs, with guitars, drums, sometimes a piano. If you're really lucky, a French horn, or a harp, or some other wonderful sound. You must have heard of it.'

She's not as funny as she thinks.

'You can tell a lot about someone from the music that they like. More than from where they live,' she explains.

'OK,' I reply. Why can't she just leave me alone?

'You see, a person chooses what music they listen to. Their place of birth is out of their hands.'

'I get it,' I respond.

I wonder what Rachel is doing right now. Probably at home, crying as she decides she's made a terrible mistake. Or, maybe she's met someone new, a guy with model looks and a great personality. I hope he can't get it up tonight. I never had that problem. Not when I was sober anyway.

'So?' she asks, jolting me back to sanity.

'So what?'

'What sort of music do you like?' she asks, laughing.

I bet she's one of those people who put on a happy face in public, but really are clinically depressed.

'I like a lot of older music,' I reply. 'Like Led Zeppelin, the Who, the Clash.'

She won't have heard of them. Probably likes Kaiser Chiefs and Keane. I swear, if she says that she likes Keane, I'm getting up and moving seats.

'I'm impressed,' she says.

'What, you like them too?' I ask.

'Of course,' she replies. 'In fact, I've got tickets to see the Who this summer.'

Now it's my turn to be impressed.

'That'll be one hell of a gig.'

'You don't say.' She grins.

I can't help but smile back.

'What's your favourite film then?' I ask her.

'Good question,' she says. 'A very important test of a person.'

'So?' I prompt.

'It would have to be *Shawshank*,' she replies.

'An excellent choice,' I remark, 'one of my favourites too.'

'What's your number one?' she asks.

'Well,' I begin, 'I'm a big fan of David Lynch's films, and Quentin Tarantino's, of course. And Alexander Payne has made some good stuff. *Sideways* – I thought that was a great film.'

'So, what's your all-time favourite then?' she presses.

'I'd have to say, *The Empire Strikes Back*.'

It's not a nice feeling, having a complete stranger laughing at you. Especially when that stranger is laughing so loudly that other people turn and stare. But I find that a huge smile is stretching across my face too.

'*Star Wars*!' she finally manages to get out. 'I would never have pegged you for a sci-fi geek.'

'I'm not,' I protest.

'I bet you changed your name as soon as you were old enough,' she says. 'Please tell me that Skywalker is your surname?'

I give her a sheepish grin.

'It is, isn't it?' she laughs.

'Of course not. My surname is Green.' I pause. 'Skywalker is my middle name.'

Again, she erupts, almost falling off her seat this time. She looks at me with tears rolling down her cheeks. She really is quite attractive.

71

'Priceless,' she says, shaking her head. 'You can't make this stuff up.'

'My parents are huge fans of the films as well,' I explain. 'They called the dog Chewie.'

This time she actually falls off her seat.

'Stop. Please stop,' she begs. 'You're killing me.'

Her wild laughter is interrupted by the driver. The train is arriving at the next station.

'This is my stop,' she says, wiping the tears from her eyes.

'I guess this is farewell then,' I say, trying to hide the regret in my voice.

'Yes, it is,' she says as she shakes my hand. 'Farewell indeed.'

And just like that she leaves, walking out of my life for ever. If only this wasn't the end.

She stops and turns.

'Luke!' she shouts. 'At least you don't like *Star Trek*.'

'Well . . .'

ONE WISH

Lisa Sanders

MY LINE MANAGER TOLD me to pick a diamond geezer to help with my research.

'Excuse me, are you a diamond geezer?' I asked the cab driver.

'Sorry, love, didn't catch that. Where to?' He turned off his radio and I could tell he was looking me over. Navy suit, low heels. Shame I had the coat on as well because it was really quite hot.

I got in, smiled and handed him a roll of money through the little window. I was nervous. It was my first time.

'What's all this for? Where do you want to go?'

I explained, saying just what I'd been told to say.

'This isn't some reality TV show, is it? You're not filming me or something?'

Surprise, then alarm, played across the diamond geezer's face.

'If this is to do with drugs, you can just get lost, all right?'

He tried to hand back the money. In another second he was going to stop the cab and ask me to get out. I tried to remember my words.

'No, no, nothing like that. Sorry for confusing you. I'm sort of a – travel agent. I need to visit some places tourists don't usually see. Off the beaten track, I suppose. Can you take me?'

'Listen, darling, for five hundred quid you're the boss. You hang on to that for now.'

He gave back the money and shrugged as if to say, 'It takes all sorts.' Then he set the meter running and pulled out into the traffic. I decided not to mention the wish part for now. It would only confuse things. After some time on a grey, wet motorway, we reached a housing estate. I was excited. I wanted to prove to my manager that I was ready for this.

'Can you let me out here, please?' I leaned forward and tapped on the glass.

'Here?'

'Yes. If you could wait for me, I'll only be a few minutes.'

I got out, joined the mothers with pushchairs and little kids. I needed to get a feel for the place. I was impressed. These people seemed well dressed. They had mango yoghurts in the fridge, and Sky TV to watch while they ate chicken tikka takeaways. Perhaps my manager had made a mistake. These people seemed to be taking care of themselves very well.

'Oi, you!' A fleshy woman whose underwear could be seen sticking out from her clothes was bearing down on me.

'You little cow! Get over here or I'll wallop you!' The woman pushed past me. She grabbed a small blonde child by the arm and dragged it towards the school gates. The child started to cry. Its legs buckled, forcing the woman to lunge down on to the pavement after it. A crowd of other parents and children flowed around them, hurrying into the school.

'Listen, Charmaine, I'm going to count to five and you'll get into school and stay there. You'll be the death of me. I wish I'd never met your dad.'

The child picked herself up and wiped away snot with the sleeve of her cardigan. In a moment she had joined the other children inside the school. Her mum, sweating visibly, walked back up the road. The woman's pain

75

THE SUN BOOK OF SHORT STORIES

was clear for me to see. She'd lost her job in the warehouse last month and had to move in with her friend Cath. Cath's boyfriend Tel kept asking when they were going to get their own place. 'I can't even get near the telly in me own home. It's not a hotel, you know,' he told Cath. She said she couldn't just kick them out, could she? Charmaine started wetting the bed and was teased at school. So her mum got more and more angry with her.

For a moment I wasn't sure what to do. My orders were to gather data for the Solutions Team to devise an Action Plan. But I couldn't just do nothing, could I?

'Excuse me.' I caught up with the woman, pulled out my card and handed it to her.

'You don't know me but I just want to say – I can grant you a wish.'

I garbled my words a bit because I'd not had a chance to think. The woman shot me a look of open hostility. She tilted my card up. It glowed a clear silver-blue in the dim morning light.

'*Heaven's Angels – Earth Action Investigation Unit?* What the bleeding hell is this? Are you trying to sell me something, because I haven't got the time, all right?'

'Um, no. Look, I can't explain it all now. I'm not really supposed to talk to you. I'm from a celestial . . . er . . . help organization. We crisis-manage problems here on earth and I am authorized to grant you one wish.'

'Are you Social Services?'

'Social what?'

'Or are you one of those church types?'

'No, actually we work directly for God. My mission is—' This wasn't going as planned. I'd surely be in trouble now. Probably never allowed to visit earth again. I needed to bring this to a close. I took a deep breath.

'Look, you don't have to understand it all. Just the fact that I have the power to grant you one wish. Anything you want, whatever you most desire, just wish it.' I smiled at her and took off my heavy coat to show her my wings.

'See?' I told her. 'I'm an angel.' I smiled again but the woman looked frozen with horror. She started running, fast, her trainers coming loose and the laces tangling round her ankles. I ran after her, desperate.

'Just make a wish!' I shouted as she sped away.

'I wish you'd leave me alone!' She turned

round and held up one finger in a gesture I didn't understand.

I put my coat back on. Walked the now-deserted pavement over to where I'd left the diamond geezer.

'Take me back, please,' I told him, exhausted.

I tried to think. There was a real problem with Heaven's new Single Wish Policy, I'd tell the line manager. True, the old Three Wishes Deal was more costly. But these days people just didn't believe in angels. Perhaps the Boss would consider launching a promotion: Two Wishes, Get the Third Free?

I wondered.

NEED TO KNOW

Kevin Tutchener

JUST ANOTHER ORDINARY FRIDAY night. A couple of drinks and enjoying a real laugh with some of my closest friends. Not what I would call long-time friends but definitely friends. Jo and Pete who I had first met about six years before. Lisa and Jimmy who knew Jo and Pete. Then there is Penny and the lovely Sally. (I had a brief affair with her seven months ago. Wouldn't mind relighting the embers of passion once more.)

And then there's me. Single male, 43, GSOH, non-smoking computer programmer with a good income, luxury flat and BMW soft-top. All seems fine but just lately I have been thinking about death and at what point this will all end. Pretty morbid, but for whatever reason it has become an issue for me. Is it because I have no family left? Except for an ex-wife somewhere in the country who I haven't heard from in over ten years. No real family left to speak of.

So I mentioned to the group that, given the chance, wouldn't we all like to know when and how we are going to die? Damn it, I would, I told them.

It was at this point that it happened. You see, everything stopped. Not stopped as in everybody shut up, but stopped as in I was the only one still moving. The music stopped, Marc Bolan once again cut down in his prime. The buzzing hum of conversation around me stopped. Penny's exclamation that she for one would not like to know came to an abrupt end. She still had a wine glass in one hand and was pointing upward with one outstretched finger.

I tried to move but couldn't. Was I in the same state as them? Could they see me as well? Did they feel the same as me? Had this happened just to me, to the group, or to everyone in the pub . . . or world! I closed my eyes and counted to ten in an attempt to shake myself from this frozen state.

Then I open them and I am here, sitting at a white wooden table in a strange room. There is no door and the walls all seem to be moving in a colourful, swirling kind of way. When I focus on one particular section it moves towards me and plays what seems to be a piece of film. A 3D scene shows a wall being knocked down by a crowd. I recognize it as the Berlin Wall. I swing to another picture and a lone figure is climbing from a silver craft, slowly and clumsily, down some steps . . . It's Armstrong about to set foot on the moon. Jesus, where am I?

'That is not important.'

I nearly fall from my chair at the sound of that voice. She is sitting opposite me, dressed in a white lacy dress and with long blonde hair. She smiles at me as she finishes her sentence and a chill runs the length of my spine. A more perfect woman I have never seen.

'Who are you?' I say with no originality at all.

'That is not important,' she repeats. She gestures towards a folder on the table in front of her. On the cover it has my name and nothing else.

'This is what you wanted. The date, the time and the manner.'

She pushes the folder towards me, still smiling.

'Now you must decide if you really want to know.'

I don't need to ask. I know what she means. But do I really want to know when I will die . . . and how? It is fine after a couple of beers, hiding behind the big talk. But now that the choice is real and no longer just a silly wish it all seems very different.

'Once you know,' she continues, 'you cannot change anything. If you try to act differently it will not matter. Anything you change will be the reason it happened anyway. It is written. It cannot be changed. Whatever is in here is what has already been decided. You cannot change anything.'

Still she smiles as she speaks. Strange warmth wraps itself around me. Memories of being comforted by my mother fill me. Other child-hood memories, like distant stars exploding and flashing across a darkened sky, come and go all within a few seconds.

'If I look, will it bring it nearer or change anything?'

'You can change nothing. It is already written.'

What should I do? To know when and how I will die, with nothing I can do to change it. What a position to be in.

I must look. It is too good an opportunity to

miss. I can control my own destiny up to that point at least.

I turn the folder to face me and look into the woman's face . . . still she smiles. I turn the cover before I change my mind. Inside is a single sheet of paper with my name on it.

Underneath is the date . . . 1st March 2007 . . . 8.47p.m. And underneath that 'Heart failure'.

I lift my head from the page, trying to take it in.

'That's today . . . that's now!'

The table and chairs have gone and I am standing facing the woman. She takes my hand and begins to lead me away.

'Remember, you can change nothing.'

The two paramedics look at each other, resigned. The doctor checks his watch and straightens up from his crouched position. He looks at each of the two green-uniformed men. 'Eight-forty-seven. That's been twenty minutes. I think we should stop. All agreed?'

The two medics both nod at their superior, who turns to the shocked group of friends. 'I'm sorry,' he says, 'we did our best. It was just his time, I guess.'

DAYLIGHT ROBBERY

Georgina Voller

THE STRONG MID-JULY HEAT blazed down upon the afternoon shoppers. The noise of the traffic, together with the humming of voices, made up the soundtrack of inner-city life. Then, quite unexpectedly, three shots rang out in quick succession. Someone screamed.

'All right, get down on the floor! Nobody move.'

The robber stood there in a Maggie Thatcher mask, pointing a gun at the teller.

'Put all the money in the bag. And be quick!'

He waved the gun around, repeating that everyone in the banking hall should lie down. The bag filled, he ran out of Carter's Bank into Holloway Road. He looked wildly up and down. His driver and so-called mate Tony was nowhere to be seen.

In a total panic, he flew across the road, making drivers swerve to miss him. Car horns blasted loudly. Everyone turned to watch the man running at top speed, mask on, gun and football bag in hand. He ran into Camden Road, past the college, and turned off into Hill Martin Road. He had no idea where he was going. North London was a long way from his own manor.

Eventually he had to stop running before his lungs exploded. Leaning against a wall, he tried to make himself think straight. To his total surprise, he realized he still had his mask on and the gun in his hand. He ripped off the mask and put it and the gun into the bag with the money.

I'll kill Tony when I get my hands on him, he thought.

Once he had his breath back, he straightened up and began to walk slowly down the road. He tried not to look worried or in a hurry. He had to get out of this area and back into his own territory as soon as possible. In the distance he could hear sirens.

He turned into Caledonian Road and started to walk towards the tube station, passing Pentonville Prison. Even though he was in a state of utter panic, he could not help smiling wryly.

What a joke, he thought, walking past a prison with a bag full of stolen money. I hope that's not where I'll end up.

More sirens now. Louder and louder. He had no idea where to go. He continued down Caledonian Road in a kind of haze. Finally, he could take no more, and pulled out his gun.

Parked by the kerb was a red Fiesta. A man was sitting at the wheel reading a newspaper.

'Get this car moving now – and don't look at me!' Brian Cadwell pointed his gun at the driver. Andy Betts did not try to argue. He simply turned on the ignition and pulled the car out into the busy traffic.

'What's this all about?' he asked.

'Shut up and drive,' Brian barked back.

As they drove towards Holloway Road Brian began to sweat. But there were no police barriers to stop them. They headed past Finsbury Park and towards Tottenham.

Finally Andy spoke again. 'Look, where do you want to go? I can't keep driving around like this all day.'

'Where do you live?' snapped Brian.

'Enfield, not far from here,' replied Andy.

'OK, take me there.'

Andy pulled the car into the main flow of traffic again. By now, Brian's state of agitation was almost too much for him. He could not wait to be off the streets. The traffic was getting heavier as they drove down the Hertford Road. It was nearly 4.30p.m., and the rush hour was beginning. Brian breathed a sigh of relief. Soon he would be safe in this bloke's house. Tomorrow he would be off and away.

Finally, the car pulled off the Hertford Road into a side turning. Brian watched as they drove down to the end of the street and stopped in front of an empty lot. He looked around for signs of a house or flat.

'I'll just check the coast is clear and open the front door,' said Andy.

Before Brian had time to react Andy was out of the car.

He's going to do a runner, thought Brian, turning around to see where Andy had gone. Then he heard the back door open. Quickly and smoothly a thin cord was slid around Brian's throat. His hands came up to try to release the pressure, but it was no good. The cord was pulled tighter and tighter as Brian began to thrash around. He was in total confusion, pain and panic. His face darkened, his lips turned blue. His feet smashed through the windscreen as he desperately tried to struggle free. Then an eerie kind of hissing noise came from his mouth and his body went limp.

Andy eased the pressure on the cord. He sat back and examined it carefully. Tiny traces of blood showed where it had cut into Brian's neck.

'What a fool,' he breathed into the dead man's ear, 'thinking you could outwit me. A common, dirty little thief like you.'

Andy got out of the car he had stolen earlier that day. He pulled the body of Brian Cadwell, bank robber and small-time con man, out of the front seat. He dragged it on to the wasteland. There he sat for quite some time, not feeling ready to leave it just yet. Finally, he walked slowly away, whistling softly under his breath.

Andrew Rory Betts was the most wanted criminal in London. He had killed nine men, including Brian, strangling them all with a fine cord. It had led the tabloids to nickname him the 'Enfield Exterminator', which made Andy rather proud. The police were at their wits' end.

Andy was having a ball.

IN TERMS OF:
AN OFFICE STORY

Steve White

IF HE SAYS 'in terms of' just one more time I think I'm going to scream, thought Joe. Slowly he squeezed the paper cup he was holding. He and the rest of the office had been listening to their manager, Cod-Face, drone on for the last two hours. Cod-Face had used the phrase 'in terms of' almost as much as footballers use 'at the end of the day'. Just one of many ways he tried to appear more intelligent than the average banana plant. It didn't work.

Joe's mind wandered back three months to when Cod-Face was introduced as their new Category Supply Chain Manager. (Or CSCM as he liked to be addressed.) At first it was as much as Joe could do not to laugh in his fish-like face. As he talked his mouth bubbled in and out in an almost hypnotic way. Joe could think only of the wet fish counter at Tesco.

Cod-Face kept droning on. 'We need to focus our efforts "in terms of" customer satisfaction.' He added the quotation marks with his fingers. That was it for Joe. The quote marks with wiggly fingers had done it for him. He could take no more. He let out an ape-like grunt.

'Joe! Everything okay? I'm not keeping you awake now, am I?' Cod-Face looked round at the rest of the team, hoping for a response to his sarcasm. Sadly for him, the team had lost the will to live within the first half-hour.

Joe used the tone of voice he usually kept for Jehovah's Witnesses. 'No, boss, just clearing my throat. Please, do carry on.'

Julie turned to him and gave a little smirk. A wave of heat passed through his body. All of a sudden he didn't feel like going straight home after work tonight. Joe smiled back. As he did he noticed her bra showing between the buttons of her shirt. Later.

Cod-Face finally brought the meeting to a close with twelve more uses of 'in terms of' in twenty minutes. 'Okay, team. It's 4.29 so let's try and maximize the final thirty-one minutes of the day. Joe, I asked you for the stock report earlier today. How's it going?'

Stunned by this outrageous request, he couldn't hold back. 'Well, chief, I would love to have done it today. But as we've been in this meeting for three hours now . . .'

'Let me cut you off there, Joe.' Cod-Face looked around at the team. 'I'm sure everyone will agree that today's meeting was highly productive. We touched on many points that will result in a more focused approach to meeting this month's targets. I'm sensing some negativity from you, Joe. Let's discuss it "off-line".' He used the finger quotes a second time.

Joe felt a bead of what could only be blood beginning to drip down his forehead. Had that vein on the side of his head burst? He reached up and discovered it was sweat. 'Okay, boss.' Joe slumped back in his chair. He prayed to a God he didn't believe in to take him away from all this. He felt defeated, deflated, and not far from doing a US postal worker special on his boss.

Before Cod-Face collared him for their 'off-line' chat, Joe popped out to the toilet. He liked the toilets at work. For a start they were much cleaner than the one at home. His feet didn't stick to the marble floor. Plus he reckoned he must save close to £50 a year on toilet roll. As Joe checked his hair in the mirror, the door to his refuge opened. It was Muzza.

'The Cod-Father has summoned you!' Muzza couldn't contain his joy. 'Don't forget to thank him for the helpful meeting, mate. Ha!'

Muzza was the closest thing Joe had to a friend at work. As Muzza had once said, he wouldn't piss on the people he worked with if they burst into flames. And Muzza was right. Most of the people Joe worked with wouldn't make it into his circle of real friends outside work.

Most workmates realize this and get on with the daily grind. They are pleasant to each other and no more. The only real problems occur when a company forces closeness on everyone through 'team building'. Joe had lost count of the number of man-hours spent bonding with his team, trying to boost morale. Why didn't they just say 'Thanks for all the hard work' and pay everyone a bit more?

He made his way back through a maze of grey panelling to reach his desk. He really hated how drab the whole place looked. The colour scheme might have been chosen especially for its de-motivational qualities. In fact, he'd started a rumour about the colour being taken out of stock at the factory after a series of suicides. Julie had really liked that story. She always seemed to laugh that little bit more when Joe was talking.

It was 4.50 when Cod-Face had finished giving him his 'off-line' pep talk. Joe had learned over the years the best way to take a telling off. 'Yes, boss.' 'No, boss.' 'Course I'm a team player, boss. In fact, I'd like to offer to brighten up the workplace a bit. I thought, maybe, a mural?'

Cod-Face swallowed it, hook, line and sinker. He even paid for the paint. Joe and Julie stayed late for weeks after that. It was the start of an office romance that didn't follow the usual pattern. Well, they're still speaking anyway.

Their colourful mural of seaweed and fish went down well with visitors. The giant cod at the centre of the painting was a real hit with all the team.

Except for the boss, of course.

READ ON THE BEACH!

Win a holiday to Barbados

Fly to the beautiful four-star **Amaryllis Beach Resort** set on a white, sandy beach on the south coast of Barbados.

For more information about the resort please visit www.amaryllisbeachresort.com. **letsgo2.com**
Holidays created by you...

HOW TO ENTER

Fill in the form below.

Name two authors who have written Quick Reads books:

1. _____

2. _____

Your name: _____

Address: _____

_____

Telephone number: _____

Tell us where you heard about Quick Reads: _____

_____

☐ **I have read and agree to the terms and conditions on the back of this page**

Send this form to: Quick Reads Competition, Colman Getty, 28 Windmill Street, London, W1T 2JJ or enter the competition on our website www.quickreads.org.uk.
Closing date: 1 September 2007

QUICK READS COMPETITION

TERMS AND CONDITIONS

1. You must be aged 18 years or older and resident in the UK to enter this competition. If you or an immediate family member works or is otherwise involved in the Quick Reads initiative or in this promotion, you may not enter.

2. To enter, fill in the entry form in the back of a Quick Reads book, in ink or ballpoint pen, tear it out and send it to: Quick Reads Competition, Colman Getty, 28 Windmill Street, London W1T 2JJ before the closing date of 1 September 2007. Or enter on our website at www.quickreads.org.uk before 1 September 2007.

3. You may enter as many times as you wish. Each entry must be on a separate form found in the back of a Quick Reads book or a separate entry on the www.quickreads.org.uk website. No entries will be returned.

4. By entering this competition you agree to the terms and conditions.

5. We cannot be responsible for entry forms lost, delayed or damaged in the post. Proof of posting is not accepted as proof of delivery.

6. The prizes will be awarded to the people who have answered the competition questions correctly and whose entry forms are drawn out first, randomly, by an independent judge after the closing date. We will contact the winners by telephone by 1 November 2007.

7. There are several prizes:
   First Prize (there will be one first prize-winner) – Seven nights' stay at a four-star resort in Barbados. The holiday is based on two people sharing a self-catering studio room with double or twin beds and includes: return flights from a London airport, seven nights' accommodation (excludes meals), use of the resort gym and non-motorised water sports. Travel to and from the London airport is not included. You will be responsible for airport transfers, visa, passport and insurance requirements, vaccinations (if applicable), passenger taxes, charges, fees and surcharges (the amount of which is subject to change). You must travel before 1 May 2008. You must book at least four weeks before departure and bookings will be strictly subject to availability. The prize-winner will be bound by the conditions of booking issued by the operator.
   Second Prize (there will be five second prize-winners) – A set of books selected by the competition Promoter including books suitable for men, women and children – to be provided by Quick Reads up to the retail value of £100.
   Third Prize (there will be one third prize-winner) – An evening in a limousine travelling around London between the hours of 6 p.m. and midnight in a limousine provided by us. You and up to five other people will be collected from any one central London point and can travel anywhere within inner London. Champagne is included. Travel to and from London is not included.
   Fourth Prize (there will be two fourth prize-winners) – £100-worth of Marks & Spencer vouchers to be spent in any branch of M&S.

8. There is no cash alternative for any of these prizes and unless agreed otherwise in writing the prizes are non-refundable and non-transferable.

9. The Promoter reserves the right to vary, amend, suspend or withdraw any or all of the prizes if this becomes necessary for reasons beyond its control.

10. The names and photographs of prize-winners may be used for publicity by the Promoter, provided they agree at the time.

11. Details of prize-winners' names and counties will be available for one month after the close of the promotion by writing to the Promoter at the address set out below.

12. The Promoter, its associated companies and agents, exclude responsibility for any act or failure by any third-party supplier, including airlines, hotels or travel companies, as long as this is within the law. Therefore this does not apply to personal injury or negligence.

13. The Promoter is Quick Reads/World Book Day Limited, 272 Vauxhall Bridge Road, London SW1V 1BA.

Quick Reads
Pick up a book today

Quick Reads are published alongside and in partnership with BBC RaW.

We would like to thank all our partners in the Quick Reads project for their help and support:

NIACE
unionlearn
National Book Tokens
The Vital Link
The Reading Agency
National Literacy Trust
Booktrust
Welsh Books Council
The Basic Skills Agency, Wales
Accent Press
Communities Scotland

Quick Reads would also like to thank the Department for Education and Skills, Arts Council England and World Book Day for their sponsorship, and NIACE (the National Institute for Adult Continuing Education) for their outreach work.

Quick Reads is a World Book Day initiative.

Quick Reads

Books in the Quick Reads series

New titles

A Dream Come True	Maureen Lee
Burning Ambition	Allen Carr
Lily	Adèle Geras
Made of Steel	Terrance Dicks
Reading My Arse	Ricky Tomlinson
The Sun Book of Short Stories	
Survive the Worst and Aim for the Best	Kerry Katona
Twenty Tales from the War Zone	John Simpson

Backlist

Blackwater	Conn Iggulden
Book Boy	Joanna Trollope
Chickenfeed	Minette Walters
Cleanskin	Val McDermid
Danny Wallace and the Centre of the Universe	Danny Wallace
Don't Make Me Laugh	Patrick Augustus
The Grey Man	Andy McNab
Hell Island	Matthew Reilly
How to Change Your Life in Seven Steps	John Bird
I Am a Dalek	Gareth Roberts
The Name You Once Gave Me	Mike Phillips
Star Sullivan	Maeve Binchy